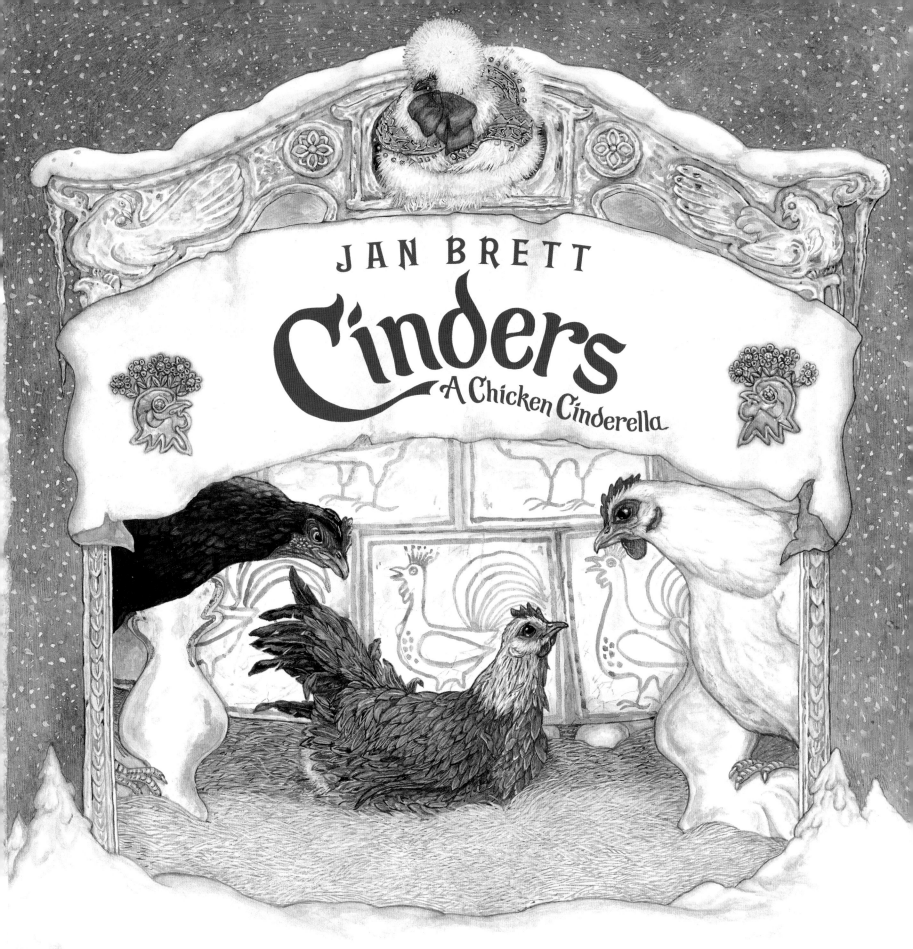

JAN BRETT

Cinders

A Chicken Cinderella

G. P. PUTNAM'S SONS

AN IMPRINT OF PENGUIN GROUP (USA) INC.

For Margaret
Lizzie, Sarah and Abby

G. P. PUTNAM'S SONS
An imprint of Penguin Young Readers Group
Published by The Penguin Group
Penguin Group (USA) Inc., 375 Hudson Street, New York, NY 10014, USA

USA | Canada | UK | Ireland | Australia | New Zealand | India | South Africa | China
Penguin Books Ltd, Registered Offices: 80 Strand, London WC2R 0RL, England
For more information about the Penguin Group, visit penguin.com

Library of Congress Cataloging-in-Publication Data is available upon request.
Library of Congress Cataloging-in-Publication Data
Brett, Jan, 1949– author, illustrator.
Cinders : a chicken Cinderella / Jan Brett.   pages cm
Summary: Cinders, the most picked upon hen in the flock, becomes the most loved by Prince Cockerel
when she arrives at his ball looking so beautiful that even her bossy sisters do not recognize her.
[1. Fairy tales. 2. Folklore.] I. Cinderella. English. II. Title.
PZ8.B675Ci 2013   398.2—dc23   [E]   2012048973

Published simultaneously in Canada.
Manufactured in China by South China Printing Co. Ltd.
ISBN 978-0-399-25783-4
1 3 5 7 9 10 8 6 4 2

Design by Marikka Tamura. Text set in Footlight MT Std.
The art for this book was done in watercolors and gouache. Airbrush backgrounds by Joseph Hearne.
The publisher does not have any control over and does not assume any responsibility
for author or third-party websites or their content.

Snow on the outside, feathered friends on the inside. Every evening, Tasha took oats to little Cinders and the other chickens in the old tower. This evening, a blizzard was raging, and Tasha had to struggle through the wind and snow to get there.

Inside, the old biddy, Largessa, and her daughters, Pecky and Bossy, pushed Cinders out of the way and ate up the oats before Cinders had any. She hid under the woodstove until Tasha lifted her gently onto her lap and fed her.

After all the chickens were cared for, Tasha tried to leave, but snow had piled up against the door. Her father was traveling and wouldn't be home until the next day, so she curled up near the warm stove.

As soon as Tasha fell asleep, a warm glow filled the room and the henhouse came to life. The chickens clucked and gossiped until Largessa, that big know~it~all, pranced out of the shadows with an invitation to a ball.

Prince Cockerel
requests the pleasure
of your company

A Fête
A Frolic
A Feathered
Fantasy

on the full moon
The Ice Palace

"Darlings," she trilled, "it will be more than a ball.
Prince Cockerel is sure to be looking for a princess bride."
She winked, and poked Pecky and Bossy. "Time to get
ready," she cackled with delight.

"Cinders! Lace my lacings and shine my slippers!" Pecky ordered.

"Bring warm water to scrub my toes," Bossy bellowed.

"Do me first!" Largessa ordered. "Trim my tail feathers and fetch my jewelry box!"

Cinders didn't know where to start. The primping and fluffing, shining and smoothing seemed to go on for hours. Would she ever have time to get herself ready for the ball? What would she wear? She began to wonder if she could even go.

The snow stopped and the moon shone a path through the window. The chickens dressed in all their finery flew off to the Ice Palace. All except Cinders. She looked down at her wet feathers and frayed wing tips and started to cry.

Suddenly, the log in the stove flared. Into the light flew
a beautiful Silkie hen Cinders had never seen before.

"I'm here to get you ready for the ball," the Silkie promised,
and she brushed Cinders with her wand.

Cinders found herself wearing a splendid silver sarafan dress.
Where ashes had covered her feathers, a silver sheen sparkled. On
her feet were the loveliest crystal slippers, and in a basket nearby,
one of her white eggs glowed like the silvery sheen of her dress.

Next, the Silkie rolled out a pumpkin. She called to the pigeons on the rafters and pulled some mice out from under the floorboards. Lastly, she summoned three ducks. Then she brushed them all with her wand.

At the palace, the ball was beginning. Largessa pushed her daughters to the front of the line and gave Pecky a shove. The prince, ever the gentleman, caught her before she fell. She looked up into his eyes, swooning the way Largessa had taught her.

As they glided away through the wintry glade toward
the Ice Palace, the Silkie called out to Cinders, "My magic will
only work until midnight. When the ice clock chimes twelve,
everything will be as before."

At the palace, the ball was beginning. Largessa pushed her daughters to the front of the line and gave Pecky a shove. The prince, ever the gentleman, caught her before she fell. She looked up into his eyes, swooning the way Largessa had taught her.

Next, the Silkie rolled out a pumpkin. She called to the pigeons on the rafters and pulled some mice out from under the floorboards. Lastly, she summoned three ducks. Then she brushed them all with her wand.

The pumpkin became a fine sleigh, the pigeons elegant footmen, and the mice, in matching livery, drove the troika of ducks, all in gilt harnesses.

Once all the guests were announced, Pecky and Bossy stayed close to the prince, keeping him away from the pretty young pullets. The door opened one more time. Everyone looked to see who the last guest could be.

Cinders stepped daintily into the ballroom, her eyes sparkling,
her head held high. No one recognized the little hen.

Prince Cockerel went forward to meet this beautiful
mystery guest. He could not take his eyes off of her.

The Silkie peeked through the window.

The prince never left her for a moment. When he crowed, she cooed.

The Silkie peeked through the window.

Prince Cockerel went forward to meet this beautiful
mystery guest. He could not take his eyes off of her.

He was the handsome prince, she the dazzling princess.

Prince Cockerel was leading Cinders onto the dance floor.

The hour grew late. Dark clouds moved in and covered the moon.
The ice clock began to chime. One, two, three, four. Cinders turned
away and flew out the door. Five, six, seven, eight. She fluttered
against the gate, losing her crystal slipper.

The pullets, the hens, the cockerels, and the roosters all wondered

The hour grew late. Dark clouds moved in and covered the moon.
The ice clock began to chime. One, two, three, four. Cinders turned
away and flew out the door. Five, six, seven, eight. She fluttered
against the gate, losing her crystal slipper.

Prince Cockerel was leading Cinders onto the dance floor.

who the graceful hen could be as she swirled around to the music.

Nine, ten, eleven, twelve. The little gray hen felt herself growing
lighter as her silver dress turned into her old frock. She was covered
in ashes just like before. The spell was broken. She flew home and
settled on her nest under the stove before the flock returned.

The next morning, the chickens twittered and clucked,
wondering who the beautiful mystery guest was and why she
had flown away. Suddenly they heard the sound of bugles,
and light from the stove lit up the tower.

In came the prince carrying a crystal slipper and Cinders's egg nestled in its basket. "I will travel to the ends of the earth until I find the one who wears this slipper and lays silvery eggs. She is my true love," crowed Prince Cockerel. "The princess of my heart."

All the hens lined up to try on the slipper. Big feet, long-toed feet, duck feet. They all tried, but not one foot fit into the dainty crystal slipper.

When Pecky jammed her foot in, her toes buckled under and
she went off in a huff. Bossy's feathered foot was so large that she
tried to hide it by pulling the slipper along with her big toenail.

The prince looked in each of the nesting boxes. He saw brown eggs, tinted eggs, speckled eggs, but not one white silvery egg. As he was turning to leave, a luminous glow in a pile of straw under the stove caught his eye.

Then he saw Cinders and beckoned her out from her nest.
She looked up at the prince and he stared into the eyes of his
lady love. He knelt down and slipped the crystal slipper onto
her foot. The prince had found his princess at last.

Outside, bells rang as a sleigh arrived at the tower. Tasha's father flung open the door, awakening his sleeping daughter.

"I thought I'd find you here among your feathered friends, Tasha," he said, revealing a handsome cockerel with a sweep of his arm.

"He will be an elegant addition to our flock," he exclaimed. "He can live on the top floor with everything he needs, and maybe some company as well. Perhaps a pretty hen you have been taking special care of!"

And from that day forward, the elegant Prince
Cockerel and Princess Cinderella ruled the roost.
And Tasha, especially on moonlit nights, tucked in
her own bed, was sure she heard the sound of music
and dancing coming from their tower.